Maud the Koala in

Fish Are Not Afraid of Doctors

by J. E. Morris

Penguin Workshop

To the staff at MGH and
healthcare professionals
everywhere—thank you!—JEM

PENGUIN WORKSHOP
An Imprint of Penguin Random House LLC, New York

Penguin supports copyright. Copyright fuels creativity, encourages diverse voices, promotes free speech, and creates a vibrant culture. Thank you for buying an authorized edition of this book and for complying with copyright laws by not reproducing, scanning, or distributing any part of it in any form without permission. You are supporting writers and allowing Penguin to continue to publish books for every reader.

Visit us online at www.penguinrandomhouse.com.

Library of Congress Control Number: 2018004225

ISBN 9780593095966   10 9 8 7 6 5 4

Fish Are Not Afraid of Doctors

by J. E. Morris

Maud went to see Doctor Susan for a checkup.

Tick
Tick
Tick

"Do you think fish are afraid of doctors?" asked Maud.

"Fish don't go to the doctor," said Mother.

"I wish I was a fish," said Maud.

"Maud, we're ready for you," said Dr. Susan.

Maud?

"She was here a second ago," said Mother.

Mother heard a small voice coming from the fish tank.

"No one here but us fish," said the voice.

"You know fish don't talk, right?" said Mother.

"Everybody follow me," said Dr. Susan.

"Everything looks good," said Dr. Susan. "All you need now is a vaccination."

"What's a vax-i-nay-shun?" asked Maud.

"It's just a teeny tiny little shot. You will hardly feel it," said Dr. Susan.

"Are fish afraid of vaccinations?" asked Maud.

"I don't think fish need vaccinations," replied Mother.

"I REALLY wish I were a fish," said Maud.

Sigh

Maud shut her eyes.

She pretended
that she had two
floppy fins!

She pretended that she had shiny red scales!

She pretended that she had a swishy, swooshy tail!

She pretended she was swimming in the deep blue sea.

She saw lots of colorful fish.
She even saw a big squiggly octopus.

She found a herd of sea turtles.
She patted their smooth, hard shells.

She met an enormous whale who
sang her a big whaley song!

"We're all done," said Dr. Susan.

"We are?" replied Maud.

"See, that wasn't so bad," said Dr. Susan.

"Have a sticker."

"You were very brave," said Mother.

"Don't you know," said Maud . . .

RECEPTION

". . . fish are not afraid of doctors!"

Note to Caregivers

No one likes getting shots, but they are sometimes necessary to keep us healthy. Fear of needles is a common childhood anxiety. And as we adults know, the actual pain is usually not nearly as bad as the fear and apprehension leading up to it.

Visualization is an effective strategy for reducing the stress and anxiety. Pretending to be in a soothing place, like swimming through a colorful coral reef, can help relieve tension and calm a child's mind. Encourage children to use all of their senses to help them visualize their happy place. What would they see, hear, smell, and feel if they were really there?

Blowing bubbles is another strategy for dealing with anxiety. Studies have shown that children who have been distracted by blowing bubbles during injections have reported less pain. Blowing on a toy pinwheel, blowing soap bubbles, or just pretending to blow bubbles are all useful distractions.

Your child will most likely never look forward to getting a shot. But by using relaxation and distraction techniques, the process can be made less painful and traumatic for everyone involved.